Beware of the Demon Headmaster

CW00847572

Read the whole Demon Headmaster series:

And coming soon:

Beware of the Demon Headmaster

((@)) - ((@))

Gillian Cross

OXFORD
UNIVERSITY PRESS

OXFORD
UNIVERSITY PRESS

Great Clarendon Street, Oxford OX2 6DP

Oxford University Press is a department of the University of Oxford.
It furthers the University's objective of excellence in research, scholarship,
and education by publishing worldwide in

Oxford New York

Auckland Bangkok Buenos Aires
Cape Town Chennai Dar es Salaam Delhi Hong Kong Istanbul
Karachi Kolkata Kuala Lumpur Madrid Melbourne Mexico City Mumbai
Nairobi São Paulo Shanghai Singapore Taipei Tokyo Toronto

With an associated company in Berlin

Oxford is a registered trade mark of Oxford University Press
in the UK and in certain other countries

British Library Cataloguing in Publication Data available

ISBN 0 19 275236 7

1 3 5 7 9 10 8 6 4 2

Typeset by AFS Image Setters Ltd, Glasgow

Printed in Great Britain
by Cox & Wyman Ltd, Reading, Berkshire

Chapter 1

Notley Castle

Hi, twin! It's gonna b gr8, said Sally's first text. She must have sent it from the train. **Dressing up first + then we get 2 fire the cannon:-) Sal**

Ben sat up in bed to read it. 'I'll text you every hour, so you know what's happening,' Sally had said. 'I promise.'

She would do it, too. She was serious about promises. Ben thought he'd better reply to the first text before the second one turned up. **Will Mrs G dress up 2?** he began. **She cud be a jailer and—**

But pressing the keys was too much effort. Even thinking was too much effort. He deleted it all and sent a really short answer instead.

Remember ur other promise. Ben

Then he flopped down miserably, pulling up the covers. He felt dreadful, and there was no one to look after him, because Mum was ill too. It looked like being a horrible day.

And he was missing the trip to Notley Castle.

... :-(.... :-(.... :-(.... :-(.... :-(.... :-(...

That was the worst thing of all. They'd spent weeks getting ready for the trip. Mrs Goddard had made everyone in the class do a different project. Sally had planned a medieval banquet for a hundred people. Ben had found out gruesome facts about the dungeon and the torture chamber and the Great Cannon. And the two of them together had copied out an old map of the castle—complete with secret passages.

Sally liked the secret passages best, but Ben loved the Great Cannon. He'd drawn three diagrams of it and made a working model—well, it *would* have worked, if Mrs Goddard had bought some gunpowder. No one in the class could persuade her to do that—but they'd all agreed on one thing. When the time came to fire the real Great Cannon—which was done every day—no one except Ben would volunteer to help. They'd let him do it.

Only he couldn't do it now, because he'd spent the whole night being sick. Mum had forced him to stay at home while Sally went dancing off to meet the others at the station. It wasn't *fair*!

He slid further down the bed and closed his eyes grumpily.

... I-O ... I-O ... I-O ... I-O ... I-O ... I-O

Just remember ur other promise, said Ben's text. Sally read it as the train pulled into the station. *Poor old Ben*, she thought. What a day to be ill. Fancy missing the castle.

They saw it as soon as they got off the train—a huge mass of grey stone standing high on a hill. It hung above the town like a heavy cloud, dark and threatening. Sally looked up at it and shuddered, thinking of bats and cobwebs and damp, mouldy dungeons.

'Don't just stand there!' Mrs Goddard snapped. 'Start walking, everyone! Our train was twenty minutes late. We ought to be up at the castle by now!'

The road went straight up the hill. They were all panting by the time they reached the top, but there was no chance to recover. As they arrived at the castle, their guide came hurrying across the drawbridge to meet them. She was dressed as a serving girl, in a long, plain dress and apron, and she was frowning at her watch.

'Quickly!' she hissed. 'Come round to the car park. You've still got to choose your

... O-Z-< ... O-Z-< ... O-Z-< ... O-Z-< ...

costumes—and the Master's talk starts in fifteen minutes. There isn't much time.'

Who's the Master? Sally thought.

But there was no time to ask questions. Their guide was hustling them across the car park, towards the Portakabin on the far side.

'Here you are!' She wrenched the door open. 'You can wear whatever you like—but choose *fast*!'

Sally expected to see a jumble of tatty dressing-up clothes, tumbled together in a shabby room. But she was completely wrong. Inside, the Portakabin was spotless and gleaming, with hundreds of clean, bright costumes hanging in order on shiny metal rails. There were long skirts and fur-trimmed gowns, suits of chain mail, and cloaks stencilled with gold—and everything looked brand-new.

For a moment, no one moved. Then Carrie Buckden said, 'I'm going to be a queen!' She clambered into the Portakabin and grabbed at a crimson dress patterned with gold.

That's beautiful, Sally thought wistfully. But it wouldn't do for her. She couldn't keep her second promise to Ben if she was wearing a dress. She had to be a knight.

... +<II-) ... +<II-) ... +<II-) ... +<II-)

Carrie had started a rush. All the other girls were darting at the rails now, pulling down costumes with long, sweeping skirts and fancy headdresses. Sally sighed. Going over to the far side of the cabin, she found a knight's costume, with a white tabard and a suit of plastic chain mail.

'Why do you want *that*?' Mrs Goddard said. 'You won't look right—not with your hair hanging down. Choose something else.'

'She's fine,' said the guide impatiently. 'There's a helmet to hide her hair.'

She pushed it into Sally's hands. Sally twisted her hair into a knot on top of her head and pulled the helmet on. It had a strip of plastic that covered her nose and made her squint.

Carrie giggled. 'You look just like Ben in that!'

The other girls started giggling too.

'That's enough silliness,' Mrs Goddard snapped. 'Hurry up and let the boys have their turn. We've only got ten minutes left.'

Time to send another text, Sally thought. She slipped out of the Portakabin and took out her phone.

Talk next then castle tour. I'm dressed

... :D ... :D ... :D ... :D ... :D ... :D ...:D ...

as a white knight—ready 4 u no what.
Fingers xed :-) Sal

The boys were very quick. As she finished
sending her message, they came bounding
out of the Portakabin. There were green
knights and red knights and yellow knights—
and one court jester. That was Laurence
Barnard, of course. He grinned at Sally and
shook his head, jingling the bells on his hat.

The guide started pushing them into line.
'Quickly now. The talk's starting in a couple
of minutes and you need to be there for the
beginning.'

She hustled them across the drawbridge,
towards the huge, arched gateway. Sally
looked up at the outside walls of the castle—
and blinked.

Where were the bats and cobwebs? Where
was the thick, tangled ivy, and the crumbling
mortar? She'd seen dozens of pictures of the
castle, looking dark and gloomy—but it
wasn't like that now. The stone walls had
been scrubbed bare and the mortar was
obviously new.

She turned round, to see if Carrie had
noticed. But Carrie was gazing up at the roof
of the great arch.

'See those slits up there?' she said. 'They

... *<):O) ... *<):O) ... *<):O) ... *<):O) ...

poured boiling oil through those — on to their enemies!'

'OWW!!' Laurence shrieked and rolled his eyes. 'THE OIL!! AARRGGGHHH!!'

The other boys started laughing and copying Laurence and Mrs Goddard turned round angrily from the ticket window. 'Stand still, all of you! We're not going into the talk until you're quiet.'

The guide looked horrified. 'You *must* go in! The Master's talk begins in one minute and forty-five seconds. Precisely.'

Mrs Goddard glared at Laurence and Carrie, who were still giggling. 'I'm not going in until everyone's calmed down.'

The guide's face froze. 'All school parties must be there for the *whole* talk,' she said. 'No one can be admitted once the presentation has begun.'

'Better for them to miss a few minutes than go in giggling,' said Mrs Goddard.

'All school parties must be there for the *whole* talk,' the guide said again. 'No one can be admitted once the presentation has begun.'

She'd repeated exactly the same words, in exactly the same stiff voice. Sally shivered. It was like listening to a robot. Laurence and

LOL .. :-)) .. LOL .. :-)) .. LOL .. :-)) .. LOL ..

Carrie stopped laughing and looked at each other uneasily.

'That's better.' Mrs Goddard gave a satisfied nod. 'Now we can go in.'

The castle clock began to strike ten. The guide ran ahead and opened a door in the left hand guard tower, beyond the arch.

'Quickly!' she said.

The bottom floor of the tower had been made into a neat little lecture theatre, with rows of seats sloping down towards a small stage. Everyone dashed in, pushing and shoving.

Sally got a place next to Laurence, in the back row, but most people were still muttering and scrambling for seats as the guide shut the door. The lights went off and for a moment the whole theatre was pitch dark. Then a spotlight came on, throwing a pool of white light on to the centre of the stage.

A tall figure strode into the light and stood looking up at the rows of seats. His eyes were hidden by dark glasses, but there was no mistaking the expression of distaste on his thin, pale face.

That expression stopped all the muttering and pushing. People sank into the nearest

8

... '\=o-o=/' .... '\=o-o=/' .... '\=o-o=/' ...

seat, wherever it was, and stared at the stage, waiting to see what was going to happen.

The tall man waited until there was complete silence and complete stillness. Then he spoke.

'I see that you are disorderly and undisciplined.' His voice was like ice. 'When I ran a school, I did not permit disorder. It is an inefficient waste of time and energy.'

What a nerve! thought Sally. *He can't say things like that. Who does he think he is?*

The tall man answered, as though he had read her mind.

'I am the Master. When I came here, this castle was inefficient too. It was dirty and old-fashioned and pointless. Now all that has changed—as you will learn soon. But first—'

He paused. Reaching up slowly, he took off the dark glasses he was wearing. For the first time, Sally saw his eyes.

They were extraordinary—huge and luminous, with deep black pupils and strange, sea-green irises. Sally had never seen eyes like them. She found herself staring into them. Staring and staring . . .

The Master stared back. When everyone was gazing into his eyes, he began to speak—

9

... ((@))-((@)) ..... ((@))-((@)) ..... ((@))-((@)) ...

and his voice was completely different now. It was soft and soothing, like a whisper. But, even in the back row, Sally could hear every word perfectly.

'First, you need to rest. I can tell that you left home early. Very, very early. No wonder you are feeling tired . . . '

What's he talking about? Sally thought. *I'm not tired—*

' . . . you are so tired and sleepy . . . ' the Master went on, in the same insistent whisper. ' . . . your eyelids are heavy . . . so heavy that you can't keep them open . . . '

But I can, Sally thought. *I can—*

' . . . so very sleepy . . . '

The voice was irresistible. So were the strange green eyes. Sally felt herself being drawn into their cold, swirling depths, sinking down and down as her eyelids began to droop and her mind blacked out. She was so, so tired . . .

(-_-)Zzzz ... (-_-)Zzzz .... (-_-)Zzzz ... (-_-)Zzzz

Chapter 2

Who is the Master?

Just before eleven o'clock, Ben's phone burbled and woke him up. It was Sally's second text. She'd sent it almost an hour ago.

Talk next then castle tour, it said. **I'm dressed as a white knight ready 4 u no what. Fingers xed :-) Sal**

Ben grinned and crossed his fingers. Then he sat up in bed. He felt much, much better. Was Mum better too—or had she gone to bed? The house was very quiet. He decided to get up and see what was going on. Pulling on some clothes, he went into the bathroom for a quick wash.

He was just cleaning his teeth when he heard his phone burble again. Another message already? He couldn't keep up with them. He rinsed his toothbrush and went to see what Sally had to say this time.

It was weird. So weird that he read it twice.

But it didn't make any more sense the second time.

It is right for the Master to rule the

... :-\ ... :-\ ... :-\ ... :-\ ... :-\ ... :-\ ... :-\

castle, it said. **Obeying the Master's instructions brings peace and order.**

Sally would never have sent a message like that. Who was it? Had Carrie been fooling around with Sally's phone? Ben snorted and sent a text to Carrie's own number.

Haha v funny. The Master sounds more SF than Middle Ages. CU 2moro Ben

Then he sent a message to ask Sally what was going on. **Who is the Master? Has Carrie gone mad?? Ben**

While he was waiting for the answers, he went to look for Mum. She was in her bedroom, fast asleep—and she looked dreadful. Ben crept away and went downstairs to make a peanut butter sandwich.

He was halfway through eating it when the next texts came through. There were two of them, from different numbers—and they were identical, except for the name.

It is right for the Master to rule the castle. Obeying the Master's instructions brings peace and order. Carrie

It is right for the Master to rule the castle. Obeying the Master's instructions brings peace and order. Sally

It had to be a joke. That was the kind of

... :-S ... :-S ... :-S ... :-S ... :-S ... :-S ...

thing that happened on a trip. Somebody said something stupid—and all the others spent the rest of the day repeating it and laughing like maniacs.

The Master's in charge!

We have to obey the Master's instructions!

Sometimes those jokes went on for weeks. That was great—if you were in at the start and you knew what the joke was all about. But if you missed the start, you could never quite catch up. Ben finished his sandwich, scowling. He was missing everything—and he wasn't even ill any more. *I could easily have gone to the castle*, he thought. He dumped his plate in the sink and went out of the kitchen.

And there was his permission form for the trip, lying on the hall table.

Mum had put it ready last night, with the money for his train fare and his entry to the castle. All he had to do was take them and walk down to the station. He could be at Notley Castle by two o'clock.

He picked up the permission form and the money and hesitated for a second. Then he slipped them into his pocket and wrote a note.

Dear Mum, I'm better now, so I've gone off to

... :-C ... :-C ... :-C ... :-C ... :-C ... :-C ...

the castle. I'll be back with Sally. Hope you're better too. Love, Ben

Should he send Sally a text, to tell her he was coming?

No. Better to creep up on them all and find out about this 'Master' joke before they realized he was there . . .

Sally and the others weren't joking. They were down in the castle dungeon.

But it's not like a dungeon, Sally was thinking. There was no mould. No green slime. There wasn't even any dirt. The floor had been scrubbed until the cobbles gleamed and the walls were painted a brilliant, spotless white. The whole place was lit by bright neon tubes that made Sally's eyes ache.

It was more like a workshop than a dungeon. And they all had work to do. Sally looked down at the heap of metal rods and bolts in front of her. They were numbered carefully, with neat, white-painted figures.

'It's complicated,' Carrie said, frowning.

'But we've got the instructions,' Sally found herself saying. 'Obeying the Master's instructions brings peace and order.'

Immediately, Carrie began to chant. 'Join

14

... +<ll-) ... +<ll-) ... +<ll-) ... +<ll-)

1/1 to 2/1 with bolt number 3. Then join 2/1 to 2/2 . . . '

It was all weird. Creepy. But Sally found herself bending down to find the right pieces — and all over the dungeon, other people were doing the same. Chanting instructions and then carrying them out, like machines with robot arms.

Laurence must be laughing, Sally thought.

Something nudged, uncomfortably, at her memory. She looked round the dungeon, trying to spot Laurence, but she couldn't see him. All the others were there, but not him. Why not? What had happened to him?

The questions nagged at her. She knew the answers. She was *sure* she did. But — she couldn't remember. And Carrie was already holding up the next two rods.

'Join 3/2 to 4/3 with bolt number 5,' she said.

Obediently, Sally bent over to find bolt number 5, and Laurence slid out of her mind.

... :-\ ... :-\ ... :-\ ... :-\ ... :-\ ... :-\ ... :-\

Chapter 3

The Dungeon

Ben got off the train—and there was the castle, on top of its hill. *You can see it from everywhere*, he thought.

It was a struggle getting up there, though. He wasn't completely better and by the time he reached the top he felt faint and dizzy. He leaned against a tree, to catch his breath.

While he was waiting there, a woman came bustling over the drawbridge. She was wearing a long dress and an apron and she disappeared into a Portakabin on the far side of the car park. When she came out again, she was wearing jeans and a T-shirt.

Maybe that's where the costumes are . . . Ben thought.

He waited while the woman hurried back into the castle. Then he glanced around. No one was watching. Going across to the Portakabin, he opened the door . . .

Five minutes later, wearing plastic chain mail and a white tabard, he crossed the

... I-O ... I-O ... I-O ... I-O ... I-O ... I-O

drawbridge, and walked into the castle. He thought he would have to pay, but the man in the ticket office just looked severely at him.

'All children in school parties must stay inside the castle walls,' he said. His voice was cold and mechanical. 'Rejoin your group at once.'

'Sorry.' Ben bobbed his head and scuttled past, through the arch.

He came out into a courtyard full of cold, bright light.

It was extraordinary. Ben had never seen anything less like a medieval castle. All the walls round the courtyard had been painted a brilliant, dazzling white and the gravel on the ground was raked absolutely smooth and even. He was afraid to walk on it, in case he made it untidy.

For a moment, he was the only person there. Then a crowd of Japanese tourists came flocking out of one of the towers. When they saw Ben, their faces lit up and they swooped towards him, waving camcorders and digital cameras. They didn't seem to speak any English, but it was obvious what they wanted. Ben smiled weakly and let them crowd round him.

17

... X-(... X-(... X-(... X-(... X-(... X-(...

While they were taking turns to be videoed and photographed with him, he scanned the castle buildings. Why couldn't he hear Mrs Goddard bellowing? Or Laurence and Carrie giggling? Where *was* everyone?

In the dungeons?

That seemed like a possibility—until he spotted the notice on the dungeon door.

WE REGRET THAT THE DUNGEON AND TORTURE CHAMBER ARE CLOSED FOR RENOVATION

Not there, then. So where were they? The towers were too small to hide a whole class and most of the rooms round the courtyard were ruined and roofless. Except for the Great Hall on the far side. They might be in there, doing a worksheet or something.

That was where the Japanese tourists headed, when they'd finally finished with Ben, so he tagged along with them. He felt less conspicuous in a crowd.

The Hall was spacious and splendid—and gleaming. The huge double doors were shiny with varnish. The carvings on the high, vaulted roof were newly painted. The vast

18

... :-\ ... :-\ ... :-\ ... :-\ ... :-\ ... :-\ ... :-\

tapestries on the walls were bright and clean and Ben could see his face in the long, polished table that ran down the centre of the room.

But Sally and the others weren't there.

Ben looked round helplessly as the Japanese tourists flooded in, chattering to each other and photographing everything. *Where do I look now?* he thought.

He was about to turn round and go back into the courtyard, when he heard the sound of hurrying feet. And then a voice, just outside the Hall door.

'I think he went in here,' said someone. It sounded like the ticket man. 'He was dressed as a white knight and he was wandering round on his own.'

'It's a girl, not a boy,' said another voice. A woman. 'She's got long hair inside that helmet.'

'She shouldn't be wandering around,' the ticket man said severely. 'All schoolchildren should be kept together. Those are the Master's orders.'

Those are the Master's orders.

Until that moment, Ben had been sure that the Master was just a joke. But the ticket man wasn't joking. There was something in

... +<ll-) ... +<ll-) ... +<ll-) ... +<ll-)

his voice that made Ben shiver. A terrible, blind obedience.

Who *was* the Master?

And why did everyone have to obey him?

Suddenly, Ben felt very frightened. While the Japanese tourists were gazing up at the carved ceiling, he lifted the corner of the nearest tapestry and slipped behind it.

He was just in time. A split second later, the ticket man walked into the Hall. Ben heard his feet on the stone floor—and then his voice.

'Have you seen someone—a schoolchild—dressed as a knight?'

Ben held his breath, even though he knew that none of the tourists spoke English. Suppose they guessed what the question meant? Or suppose the ticket man spotted a bulge in the tapestry? What then?

Ben shrank backwards, trying to be invisible. Flattening himself against the wall behind him.

Only it wasn't a wall.

He was expecting stone, or wooden panelling, but the surface behind him was flat and smooth and cold. Like glass.

* * *

... <=-O ... <=-O ... <=-O ... <=-O ...

Sally and Carrie had bolted all their metal rods together. Whatever they'd made was taller than they were, and very solid. It looked like some kind of framework.

They straightened up and stood quietly, waiting to see what would happen next. Gradually, two by two, all the others did the same. Within fifteen minutes, the whole dungeon was still and silent.

And then, way up at the top of the steps, a key turned in the heavy dungeon lock. The great dungeon door creaked open, and feet came padding down the steps. Looking up, Sally saw their guide—dressed in jeans and a T-shirt now—followed by the man from the ticket office.

The two of them stood on the bottom step, scanning the dungeon, their eyes flicking from face to face. When they reached Sally, they stopped. The guide looked sideways at the ticket man, raising an eyebrow.

'That one?'

The ticket man nodded. 'That's the one.'

For a horrible moment, Sally thought they were going to run down the steps and grab her, but they didn't. The guide studied her face and relaxed visibly.

'All schoolchildren are together,' she said.

The ticket man nodded again. 'The Master's orders have been obeyed.'

For an instant he almost looked pleased.

Then the dungeon door creaked again. Immediately, he stiffened and whirled round, looking up at the top of the steps. And everyone copied him. Every head in the dungeon turned, tilting back to see who had come in.

It was the Master.

He stood at the top of the steps, gazing down into the dungeon. His pale face was expressionless and his eyes were hidden behind his dark glasses. Sally felt cold and frightened. What was he going to do?

He began to walk down the steps, glancing from side to side of the dungeon and scanning the strange shapes made by the newly-assembled rods. Once or twice he gave a small, satisfied smile. The guide and the ticket man flattened themselves against the wall to let him by and he swept past without even looking at them.

He didn't speak until he was down in the dungeon itself. Stopping at the bottom of the steps, he looked round once more, to be sure that everyone was staring at him.

Then he said, 'Who am I? And what is this place?'

... '\=0-0=/' .... '\=0-0=/' .... '\=0-0=/' ...

Sally found herself answering with everyone else. Exactly in time.

'You are the Master and this is the castle. It is right for the Master to rule the castle. Obeying the Master's instructions brings peace and order.'

'That is correct,' the Master said coldly. 'Today, I rule the castle. By tomorrow—' He paused for a moment and gave a chilly smile. 'By tomorrow I shall be ruling this whole town. Everyone in it will obey my orders.'

That's ridiculous, said a little voice at the back of Sally's mind. *If Laurence was here, he'd be laughing his head off.*

But Laurence wasn't there—and she didn't know where he was.

'Tomorrow I shall rule this town,' the Master repeated. 'It will be an example of logical, efficient government. Within six months, people will be begging me to run the whole country.'

Sally caught her breath. *He's crazy. He wants to take over everything. We can't let him—*

But there was no time to protest. The Master reached up and took off his dark glasses and his extraordinary, sea-green eyes dominated the dungeon.

'What will I be doing by tomorrow?' he said.

... ((@))-((@)) ..... ((@))-((@)) ..... ((@))-((@)) ...

And Sally heard herself answer, in unison with everyone else, 'By tomorrow, you will be ruling the town.'

'And in six months?'

The answer came without any hesitation, from everyone. 'In six months, you will be ruling the country.'

The Master gave another small, cold smile. 'Precisely. I am going to take over the country—and this afternoon all of you will help me take the first step.'

No! Sally struggled to stay in control of her mind. *I'm not going to help you!*

But it was hopeless. The Master's face swam in front of her. His huge green eyes stared straight into hers. She felt her mind blur and cloud over until she wasn't aware of anything except his voice.

'Listen carefully to my instructions . . . '

... ((@))-((@)) ..... ((@))-((@)) ..... ((@))-((@)) ...

Chapter 4

The Secret Passage

When the ticket man finally left the Hall, Ben took a long, deep breath. His mind was boiling with questions.

Who is the Master?
How does he get everyone to obey him?
Is Sally all right?
Where is she?

He was pretty sure he knew the answer to the last one. What had the ticket man said? *All schoolchildren should be kept together.* If that was true, there was only one place where Sally and the others could be, if they were still in the castle. They had to be in the dungeon.

Still hiding behind the tapestry, Ben rang Sally's number—and he got the answer he expected. *The phone you are calling may be switched off. Please try later.*

It wasn't switched off. He was sure of that. It was underground, too deep for any signal to reach. Sally and the others were in the dungeon all right—and he had a horrible feeling they were locked in.

He took a long, deep breath, to stop himself

... (0-< ... (0-< ... (0-< ... (0-< ... (0-<

shaking. He was very frightened now, but he knew what he had to do. Thanks to the map that he and Sally had drawn . . .

He had to get into the kitchen without being spotted. Sliding along the smooth glass behind him, he peered round the edge of the tapestry. The Japanese tourists looked as though they were leaving. Great! If he was lucky, he could use them as cover.

It worked like a charm. As the tourists spread across the courtyard, Ben scuttled through the Hall door, turned right, and ducked behind the ruined wall of the kitchen. His feet sounded very loud on the gravel, so he hurried towards the fireplace at the far end of the kitchen. He wanted to get there while the chattering tourists were still close enough to mask the noise of his steps.

The fireplace was a huge stone cave, big enough for ten men to stand in. Its back wall was blackened by cooking fires, but the fires were out now—and, if Ben's research was right, that black wall didn't go all the way up into the chimney.

He glanced round to make sure that no one was watching. Then he began to hunt for

... <=-O ... <=-O ... <=-O ... <=-O ...

footholds in the blackened stone. *Don't expect too much,* he told himself. Mrs Goddard said the secret passages were just a legend. And even if she was wrong, this one might have collapsed years ago. Or been blocked up.

In a few seconds he was out of sight, hidden in the chimney. He hauled himself into the darkness, clinging to little ledges in the stonework. When he was about fifteen feet up, the wall sloped back abruptly — and stopped. Above his head, the real back wall sloped forward to take over, going on up the chimney.

From below, the whole thing looked like one continuous stretch of blackened stone, but Ben could feel the gap between the two walls. He slithered over the top of the false back wall and climbed down the other side of it, into the darkness.

It was twice as far going down.

When he finally reached a solid floor, he was fifteen feet below ground. He couldn't see a thing, but he knew exactly where he was. Mrs Goddard had made him redo the castle map three times, until it was tidy enough. He could have drawn it in his sleep.

This secret passage ran right under the courtyard, to the torture chamber and the dungeon. Keeping his hand on the wall, Ben picked his way over the stony floor, trying not to make any noise.

Finally, he came to a dead end.

At least, it felt like a dead end—but he knew better. The Notleys had built the tunnel to make sure that they could never be imprisoned in their own dungeon. And whoever designed it had worked the fireplace trick twice. The dead end was a second dummy wall at the back of an underground fireplace.

In the torture chamber.

Ben listened for a moment. There was no sound coming from beyond the dummy wall. Slowly he ran his hands over the surface, finding the little ledges that had to be there. Then he started to climb.

At the top he stopped, straddling the false wall and peering down into the fireplace. He couldn't see a thing. The torture chamber was pitch dark. Holding his breath, he listened hard and caught the sound of distant voices. He couldn't make out what they were saying, but he thought they were in the dungeon, on the other side of the torture chamber.

Gripping the wall, he swung his other leg over the top and began to climb down, moving very slowly and quietly. He was getting tired now. The climbing took a lot of concentration and his arms and legs were aching. When he finally reached the bottom, he lay down flat in the fireplace, waiting for his heart to stop pounding. He didn't want to move another step.

But he had to find Sally.

Raising himself on his hands and knees, he started crawling out of the fireplace. He was just about to stand up when he put out his hand—and touched a leg.

There was a peculiar sound, like a muffled moan. Then the leg moved. Ben snatched his hand away, breathing hard.

He could hear someone else breathing too. With a shaking hand, he reached forward again through the air, and his fingers met cloth. Rough, damp cloth, stretched very tight. Above that was a nose which twitched away from him, with a jangle of tiny bells.

Ben didn't understand the bells, but he knew what the cloth was.

'Keep still,' he breathed. 'I'll try and undo the gag. OK?'

Another moan—quieter this time. Ben found the knot and began to work at it. It was pulled very tight and he broke two finger nails, but in the end it came loose and he unwound the gag.

'Is that—Ben?' said a hesitant voice.

It was Laurence.

Sally looked round the dungeon and blinked. It felt like waking up—but why would she have been asleep?

'What happened?' she said.

Beside her, Carrie blinked too, turning her head. 'We are waiting for the Master's signal,' she said in a dull, mechanical voice. 'We have to wait here until he tells us to start.'

All around them, other people were blinking and stretching, and Sally could hear the same answer being whispered over and over again. *We are waiting for the Master's signal.*

How long would they have to wait? Sally's legs were aching, but there was no room to sit down. Now that all the rods were bolted together, there was hardly room to stand.

'I'm going to find some more space,' she said.

Carrie shook her head. 'You'll be lucky.'

But Sally had spotted the door on the far side of the dungeon—the one that led into the torture chamber. It would be dark on the other side of that door, but there ought to be space to sit down. She began to wriggle towards it, edging people out of the way and squeezing past bits of framework.

The door was slightly ajar. When she reached it, she grabbed the handle—

But she couldn't move the door.

There was nothing to stop her. The door wasn't stuck. There was no electric current, no invisible force field. It was her mind that stopped her. It wouldn't let her go out of the dungeon.

She stared down at her hand as it gripped the door handle. *I don't understand,* she thought.

Then someone tapped her on the shoulder. She looked round and saw Mrs Goddard.

'What are you doing, Sally?' Mrs Goddard said.

'We are waiting for the Master's signal,' Sally heard herself say mechanically. 'We have to wait here until he tells us to start.'

... :-S ... :-S ... :-S ... :-S ... :-S ... :-S ...

Chapter 5

The Master's Instructions

'It was weird,' Laurence said. His head was close to Ben's and he was talking in a fast, nervous whisper. 'We went into this lecture theatre. I *thought* we were going to have a talk about the castle.'

'And?' muttered Ben.

'A man came in and started telling us how tired we were. And—everyone's eyes closed. I thought it was some kind of game, so I . . . I—' Laurence's voice wobbled and faded away.

'What did you do?' whispered Ben.

'I—' Laurence swallowed. 'I *snored*.'

Ben had to bite his finger to stop himself laughing. He knew just what kind of snore it would have been. Something very loud and piglike. 'The man didn't like that?'

'He pointed at me,' Laurence muttered. 'And three other men came and lifted me out of my seat. Over everyone's head. I was shouting for help, but the others didn't even open their eyes. It was as if—' He turned his head away.

'As if what?' Ben whispered urgently.

(-_-)Zzzz ... (-_-)Zzzz .... (-_-)Zzzz ... (-_-)Zzzz

'Laurence, you've got to tell me. Or we'll never understand what's going on.'

Laurence was silent for a moment. Then he spoke again, very softly. 'They were all hypnotized or something. As if he'd taken their minds over. It was *horrible*.'

Hypnotism.

Ben nodded slowly. It was horrible—but it made sense. That strange, blind obedience. And the same words repeated over and over again. *It is right for the Master to rule the castle. Obeying the Master's instructions brings peace and order.*

The Master hypnotized people. And anyone who didn't get hypnotized—like Laurence—was put out of the way. Ben felt sick.

'They dumped me down here in the dark,' Laurence mumbled. 'I've been here for *hours*.'

'What about the others?' Ben whispered. 'Are they through in the dungeon?'

'I think so.'

'Let's take a look.' Ben turned towards the chink of light that showed where the door was. 'Coming?'

There was another jangle of little bells.

Ben's heart thudded. 'What *is* that?'

'Sorry,' mumbled Laurence. 'Forgot I was wearing a jester's hat. I was shaking my head.'

33

... *<):O) ... *<):O) ... *<):O) ... *<):O) ...

Ben was annoyed. 'You're *not* coming?'

'I can't,' Laurence hissed. 'I'm tied to the wall.'

'Why didn't you say so?'

Impatiently, Ben felt around to find the rope. Laurence's wrists were tied to a metal ring in the wall and it took fifteen minutes and three more broken nails to get the knots undone.

Finally, Ben pulled the rope away. 'Let's get going. And don't shake your head about!'

They crawled across the torture chamber, to the big, studded door. It was open just wide enough to peep through. Lying flat on the floor, they peered out into the dungeon.

Ben had a glimpse of bright white light, reflected off bright white walls—and he saw Mrs Goddard's ankles.

She was standing right on the other side of the door, blocking out most of the view, but it was her all right. And he could see some of the others beyond her. They seemed to be talking softly but he couldn't catch any of the words.

He was just wondering whether he dared to prod Mrs Goddard, to attract her attention, when everything changed suddenly. The

34

talking stopped and people turned away from him, to face the dungeon steps.

Someone was coming down those steps.

Someone with hard, heavy shoes was walking down slowly, step by step, in silence. Ben couldn't see who it was, but Laurence was at a slightly different angle and he gulped.

'It's him!' he whispered, straight into Ben's ear. 'It's the man who hypnotized everyone.'

The Master. Ben's heart started beating like a drum. He held his breath, listening hard.

The Master's voice, when it came, was brisk and cold. 'Who am I? What am I going to do today?'

Everyone in the dungeon answered, loud and clear. 'You are the Master. Today you are going to take over the town.'

WHAT? Ben couldn't believe his ears. That had to be a joke.

But no one laughed. Everyone went on listening as the Master gave instructions.

'At five o'clock precisely, you will leave this dungeon,' he said. 'The boys will take the framework up on to the north side of the battlements and assemble it there. I have allotted seven minutes for that. Afterwards, I shall need one boy for another job.'

35

... ((@))-((@)) ..... ((@))-((@)) ..... ((@))-((@)) ...

Ben moved his head to peer past Mrs Goddard's ankles. He could see some complicated constructions made of metal rods. That must be the framework.

The Master was still talking.

'The girls will go to the Great Hall and fetch the large video screen from behind the left hand tapestry. I have allotted nine minutes for carrying it up on to the battlements and fixing it to the framework. The screen must be securely in place by ten past five.'

So *that* was what he'd found behind the tapestry! It was all Ben could do not to gasp. Why would anyone want a video screen *that* big? And what had it got to do with taking over the town?

There was no explanation. The Master was giving instructions to the teachers now.

'All the adults will ensure that this happens smoothly and deal with anyone who tries to interfere. Is that clear?'

From above Ben's head, Mrs Goddard chanted with all the other teachers:

'We will deal with anyone who tries to interfere.'

'Excellent,' the Master said coldly. 'Now I am going to leave. You will forget all this,

36

... :-O ... :-O ... :-O ... :-O ... :-O ... :-O

until you hear the castle clock strike five. Then you will carry out my instructions.'

He began to climb back up the steps. No one made a sound until the door creaked shut behind him. Then people began to chatter, as though nothing had happened.

Laurence whispered into Ben's ear again. 'What do we do? Tell them what's going on?'

Ben frowned. 'We don't *know* what's going on. And if we try and interfere—the teachers will *deal with us*. I don't like the sound of that.'

'But we've got to do *something*,' Laurence said desperately.

'Let's begin by getting out of here. Come on.' Ben turned round and started to wriggle back to the fireplace—and the secret passage.

Sally was squashed into a corner beside the door. She didn't know why they were spending so long down in the dungeon, but it was really boring. Turning her back on the others, she pulled out her phone and began a new text to Ben.

Hope U R better. Dungeon full of

... I·O ... I·O ... I·O ... I·O ... I·O ... I·O

bits of metal and BAD air. :-[Am remembering my promise. The cannon will be fired at 5.15 pm. Sal

There was no signal down in the dungeon, but she could send it as soon as they were outside again—whenever that was.

... :-C ... :-C ... :-C ... :-C ... :-C ... :-C ...

Chapter 6

'I shall need one boy . . .'

The secret passage seemed even darker this time. Ben went steadily, because he knew the ground was uneven, but Laurence kept trying to run—and falling over.

'Slow down,' Ben said, the third time he pulled him up.

'But we've got to hurry!' Laurence said. 'We have to stop the Master—or he'll hypnotize everyone in the whole town.'

'All at once?' Ben almost laughed. 'What's he going to do? Cram them into the lecture theatre?'

'They only have to stare into his eyes for a second,' Laurence said. 'You didn't see how quick it was.'

'But there are thousands of people in the town. They can't all stare into his eyes at once. Not unless—'

Not unless he has gigantic eyes . . .

Ben stopped dead and a long, cold shiver went down his spine.

Laurence stopped too. 'What's the matter?'

'I know what the video screen is for,' Ben said grimly. 'If it's up on the battlements, everyone in the town will be able to see it, won't they? And if it's showing the Master's face—'

He didn't need to spell it out. Laurence gasped and grabbed his arm.

'We've got to stop him,' he said. 'They won't stand a chance. But how—?'

'We can get to the Great Hall before the girls,' Ben said grimly. 'And smash the video screen.'

Laurence didn't hesitate. 'Let's go!'

They raced along the secret passage. They were at the end in a couple of minutes—but it took ten more minutes to climb the false wall at the back of the kitchen fireplace.

As they reached the top, they heard the clock begin to strike five. Immediately, the courtyard filled with the sound of tramping feet. Ben threw himself down the other side of the wall, but it was too late. Before he hit the ground, a line of girls came marching across the courtyard, with Mrs Goddard behind them. By the time he reached the front wall of the kitchen, they were going into the Hall.

Sally was the last one. She stopped at the door, fumbling with her phone.

'Don't waste time!' Mrs Goddard snapped.

.. O-Z-< ... O-Z-< ... O-Z-< ... O-Z-< ... O-Z-<

'The Master's instructions must be obeyed.'
She pushed Sally into the Hall.

Ben waited impatiently for the text that
Sally had just sent. It took ten seconds and
when it did it looked useless.

**Hope U R better. Dungeon full of
bits of metal and BAD air. :-[Am
remembering my promise. The cannon
will be fired at 5.15 pm. Sal**

What was all that about? Didn't she realize
what was going on? Didn't she even *suspect*?
Ben was so disappointed that he almost missed
the important piece of news in the text. He
was putting his phone away before it hit
him.

The cannon will be fired at 5.15 p.m.

That wasn't right. All the books said that
the cannon was fired at half past two—in
memory of the birth of Fulke Notley in 1587.
Why was it so late today?

Ben glanced up at the cannon, on the
battlements—and suddenly he had an idea.

'I know how we can do it!' he hissed. 'I
know how we can stop the Master!'

But he needed something heavy. What
could he use? He looked round frantically—
and saw the jester's hat on Laurence's head.
He snatched it and knelt down on the gravel.

... *<):O) ... *<):O) ... *<):O) ... *<):O) ...

'What are you doing?' Laurence said.

But Ben didn't have time to explain. He was too busy scooping handfuls of gravel into the big, floppy jester's hat.

The video screen was huge and heavy, and very uncomfortable to carry. They held on all round the edge and carried it horizontally as they crossed the courtyard. By the time they reached the castle wall, Sally's arms were aching. There were modern stone steps leading up on to the battlements on the north side, and she climbed them backwards, bending double to keep hold of the screen.

On the battlements themselves, there wasn't room to hold the screen flat. Sally let go and edged in among the boys, to give the other girls room to get up. They reached the framework and began to manoeuvre the screen into place.

It was a moment or two before Sally realized that the Master was watching.

He was standing in the tower at the corner of the battlements, following every movement. In one hand he was holding a metal box, and in the other he had a long stick. As the girls began to tighten the clamps that held the

... >[]I .... >[]I .... >[]I .... >[]I .... >[]I ....

screen, he took a step towards the crowd of boys. His eyes flicked over them. Green knights, red knights, yellow knights—and Sally.

He's looking, Sally thought. *He's looking for someone—*

Her first reaction was to shrink back, out of his way. But suddenly—just in time—she caught sight of the big clock over the gateway. It was almost quarter past five.

Nearly time to fire the cannon, Sally thought.

And suddenly, in a flash, she realized what the Master wanted. He'd come to choose someone to fire the cannon. And he had to choose her! That was what she'd promised Ben. *If you're not there—I'll do it.*

As the Master began to speak, she was ready, poised on tiptoe. She'd been waiting for this, all day.

'The Great Cannon will be fired at exactly five fifteen,' the Master said briskly. 'One of you will do it—a knight.'

Sally felt the boys move forward eagerly, ready to be chosen. But she didn't wait for the Master to choose. She stepped forward smartly.

'I'll do it!' she said.

Some of the boys began to mutter, but

43

... +<ll-) ... +<ll-) ... +<ll-) ... +<ll-)

Carrie heard Sally's voice and looked round from the screen. *So that's why you couldn't wear a dress*, her expression said. She interrupted, before any of the boys could speak out loud.

'It's only fair!' she said. 'The white knight should fire the cannon.'

For a second, it hung in the balance. Then the boys all took a step back, leaving Sally standing on her own, in front of the Master.

He looked steadily at her. She couldn't tell what he was thinking, because the dark glasses hid his eyes, but after a moment he nodded.

'You will do as well as anyone else,' he said. 'Follow me.'

He set off round the battlements. There was a square tower at each corner, and he led Sally through two of them to reach the cannon, halfway along the south wall. It was exactly opposite the screen, pointing away from it over the deep dry moat.

The Master looked at the gleaming metal for a second. 'The Great Cannon of Notley Castle,' he murmured. 'The weapon that will ensure my victory.'

He seized the huge barrel of the cannon and tilted it upwards. Taking a key out of his pocket, he unlocked the metal box he had brought and tipped some dark powder into

44

'\=o-o=/' .... '\=o-o=/' .... '\=o-o=/' ...

the mouth of the cannon. Then he put the box down and pulled a wad of cloth out of his pocket. Dropping it in on top of the powder, he rammed it down hard with his stick.

Sally had seen Ben's diagrams. She knew what the Master was doing. He had put in gunpowder, but no cannon ball. It was going to be a blank shot.

The Master lowered the barrel of the cannon until it was level, pointing out over the battlements. Then he pulled out the little bung near the back, opening up a small hole. He trickled a handful of gunpowder into that, filling it completely.

That's the fuse, Sally thought. *All it needs now is something to light it.*

The Master took out a box of matches.

'It is exactly twelve minutes past five,' he said smoothly. 'You must stay beside the cannon. At a quarter past five, the castle clock will strike once. When it does, you will light the powder in the little hole. Is that clear?'

Sally nodded.

'When people hear the shot—' a small, triumphant smile crossed the Master's face, '—they will look up and wonder why it is

45

late.' His smile twisted scornfully. 'And their curiosity will deliver them into my hands.'

Laying the matches on top of the metal box, he turned away, towards the nearest tower. Sally heard him march down the stone steps and a second later, he emerged into the courtyard. The guide and the ticket man were down there, setting up floodlights and a camera.

Sally was watching them when a voice hissed at her from the corner tower, beyond the cannon.

'Psst! Sal!'

She looked up sharply. It was Ben.

'Over here!' he whispered.

Sally tried to take a step towards him—but she couldn't. 'I must stay beside the cannon,' she found herself saying. 'At a quarter past five, the castle clock will strike once. When it does, I must light the powder.'

'But *I* want to fire the cannon,' Ben said.

Sally heard her voice answering, like a robot's. 'I have my instructions. Obeying the Master's instructions brings peace and order.'

... :-. ssshhh ... :-. ssshhh ... :-. ssshhh ...

Chapter 7

The Great Cannon of Notley Castle

Ben couldn't believe it. 'The Master's *evil*, Sal. He's plotting to take over the town.' He pointed into the courtyard. 'Look.'

It was almost dark, but the courtyard was brightly lit, with its white walls gleaming. The Master was standing in front of the camera. A little monitor showed his face — and a long cable ran from there to the screen on the battlements.

Sally's face didn't change. 'Today, the Master rules the castle. Tomorrow he will rule the town. Within six months, people will be begging him to run the whole country.'

'That's *crazy*,' Laurence said. 'He just wants to take over everything.'

The hands on the castle clock reached a quarter past five and the clock struck, with a shuddering *boom*. Immediately, Sally bent down and picked up the matches.

'Let's rush her,' Laurence said.

'No use,' Ben said. 'Look — she's already lit the match.'

Sally touched the match to the little hole

47

... >[]I .... >[]I .... >[]I .... >[]I .... >[]I ....

full of gunpowder. Down in the courtyard, the Master looked up and gave a small, approving smile.

The next second, there was a huge, sonorous, ear-splitting **BOOM!!** a thousand times louder than the noise of the clock. The Great Cannon rumbled, and the wad of cloth in its barrel shot out over the battlements and dropped into the dry moat.

Down in the town, people heard the noise and glanced at their watches. What was going on? Stepping out into the street, they looked up at the castle—and saw the huge screen.

'Now,' said the Master.

The woman in jeans fiddled with a couple of switches and light flooded out from the far side of the huge screen. Ben saw the glare— and in the little monitor he saw what the big screen was showing.

The Master's face was gazing from the battlements, blown up to a nightmare size. His green eyes dominated the town.

Then he began to speak. And his voice rang out like thunder.

'People of Notley, it has been a long, tiring day. You must be feeling sleepy . . .'

Laurence was trying to say something, but

the noise from the Master's voice was so loud that Ben couldn't hear. He leaned closer as Laurence said it again.

' . . . must stop him . . . that's how he does it . . . can't we rush . . . ?'

Ben looked down at the courtyard. The Master was concentrating on the camera, but the ticket man and the woman were watching the battlements. He shook his head.

Laurence looked wretched. 'Maybe . . . persuade Sally . . . '

He's mad, Ben thought. *She won't hear a word I say. I can't—*

Then he remembered his phone. He waved it at Sally and then tapped in a message, at top speed.

Everyl promised I cud fire the cannon if I was here. And I AM. I'm comin 2 fire it.

It took the message a few seconds to reach Sally, and all the time the Master's voice was crooning on and on, filling the air above the town.

'You're all so tired . . . so very, very tired . . . '

Hurry up! Ben thought. *There's not much time left!* He held his breath as Sally reached for her phone. She replied instantly.

49

I've already fired it. U R 2 late + the Master will C U.

Ben was ready for that. His fingers flew over the buttons.

Hide Bhind the cannon + I'll come + fire it again. U PROMISED!

Sally *always* kept her promises. He was banking on that.

She read the message and frowned, glancing down into the courtyard. Ben saw her watching the guide and the ticket man, waiting for their eyes to flick past her.

She let them see what they expected—a white knight, standing still and upright on the battlements, with his shadow falling across the dark bulk of the cannon. Then, the moment they looked away, she ducked down behind the cannon.

'NOW!' Ben hissed, into Laurence's ear. The two of them raced out to the cannon as the Master's voice grew smoother and gentler.

' . . . you can hardly keep your eyes open . . . '

Ben grabbed the barrel of the cannon. 'Swing it round! Quickly!'

They leaned against the huge metal shape, and it swivelled right round on its metal base.

.. **O-Z-<** ... **O-Z-<** ... **O-Z-<** ... **O-Z-<** ... **O-Z-<**

Now it was pointing inwards, across the courtyard, angled slightly upwards, to aim at the back of the huge screen.

Next time the ticket man glanced along the south side of the battlements, everything looked the same as before. A white knight stood still and upright, with his shadow falling across the dark bulk of the cannon.

Ben stayed motionless until the ticket man looked away again. Then he tilted the cannon up and hissed down at Laurence and Sally.

'The metal box!'

They passed it up and he tipped nearly all the remaining gunpowder into the cannon.

'Now the hat!'

Laurence hoisted up the jester's hat that he and Ben had brought on to the battlements with them. They'd filled it with gravel, with Ben's school tie tied round the top to hold it shut. It was very heavy. Ben slid it into the cannon, on top of the gunpowder, and pushed it right in with the Master's stick.

' . . . you are fast asleep,' the Master's voice was still crooning over the loudspeakers. ' . . . very, very fast asleep . . . '

But, as Sally held up the matches, it

51

changed suddenly. The crooning stopped, and the Master began to speak briskly.

'Now you will do exactly as I tell you!'

'We're too late!' Laurence said desperately.

Ben wasn't going to give up. He swung the barrel of the cannon down, to point at the back of the screen, and tipped the last spoonful of gunpowder into the fuse hole. Then he took the matches.

'These are my instructions!' The Master said, his voice echoing across the town.

He paused for a second—and in that instant of silence Ben lit a match and yelled across the courtyard, as loudly as he could.

'Get away from the screen!'

On the opposite side of the battlements, everyone scattered as he touched the match to the fuse hole. A split second later, with a gigantic BOOM! the Great Cannon fired for the second time. It shot the loaded jester's hat across the courtyard, straight into the back of the screen.

Down in the town, people were waiting for the Master's instructions. They saw his huge face totter for a second and then pitch forward, crashing on to the stone battlements. With a terrifying crash, it splintered into a

.......)))))))))((((O<<<<<<*< .... >[]| ....

million fragments that showered outwards, catching the light like snowflakes.

There was a moment's stunned silence.

The Master roared with fury and spun round, glaring straight up at Ben. For the first time, Ben found himself gazing into those huge green eyes—and they were scorching with rage. He felt himself grow dizzy and start to black out. *I can't, I can't*—

He was almost unconscious when he heard the sound of shouting voices. Thousands of voices. And thousands of feet, thundering up the hill towards the castle. Suddenly— mercifully—the terrible green eyes turned away from him, leaving him free to slump sideways, against the cannon.

The Master was striding across the courtyard. Without a backward glance, he disappeared into the Great Hall.

'What's he doing?' Laurence said.

Ben leaned on the cannon, recovering. 'Escaping,' he said faintly. 'That's where the other secret passage is. The one that leads outside the castle.'

Sally looked puzzled. 'But what's he escaping *from*?'

Ben pulled himself upright and pointed towards the castle gateway. 'Listen,' he said.

53

'They're coming up from the town. Can't you hear what they're shouting?'

It was getting louder every second. 'Smash the face! Smash the face!'

'They think that's what the Master meant.' Ben took a deep breath. 'He said, "*These are my instructions*" — and then the screen broke, so they think they have to smash his face.'

Sally shivered. 'Will he make it? Will he get away?'

'Let's see.' Ben turned away from the courtyard and leaned over the battlements, peering down into the moat.

Just as the first of the townspeople clattered on to the drawbridge, there was a shuffling, dragging noise in the darkness below the cannon. A shadowy figure came crawling out of the drainage pipe at the bottom of the castle wall and Ben caught a whiff of damp, mouldy air.

'That's him,' he said.

The figure stood for a second, staring up at the castle. Then it plunged down the slope into the moat — just in time. The townspeople were racing through the great archway and into the courtyard.

'Turn round!' Sally hissed at Ben and

... X-(... X-(... X-(... X-(... X-(... X-(...

Laurence. 'Don't let them guess where he's gone!'

Ben stared into the dark. *Are we just going to let him get away?* he thought. *What will he do next?*

'Ben!' Sally said urgently.

Ben turned round and saw the townspeople swarming into the castle—and he knew Sally was right. They couldn't show those people where the Master had gone. That was the sort of thing *he* would have done. If they behaved like that—he would have won after all. He turned away, heading for the spiral stair that led down to the courtyard.

'Hang on,' Sally said. 'Let's send Mum a text to say we're OK. In case this gets on the News.'

Laurence grinned. 'I'll do it.' He took the phone out of Ben's pocket and started a message.

The townspeople had begun to mill around in the courtyard, running out of steam. Some of them had noticed the white paint on the ancient stonework and they were looking furious.

'It's going to be all right,' Ben said. 'When they realize they can't find the Master, they'll probably start scrubbing the walls.'

55

... :V ... :V ... :V ... :V ... :V ... :V ... :V ...

Sally grinned, and leaned over to read the text that Laurence was about to send.

It said **Hav smashed video screen, fired cannon + defeated evil Master. Back 4 T love—**

'Are you mad?' Sally snatched the phone. 'We can't send *that*! Mum's *ill*!'

She deleted it all and sent a safe message.

C U 4 T B4 8 + we R cookin 4 U 2nite love B + S

Baffled by some of the text symbols in this book?
Try looking on
www.oup.com/uk/demonheadmaster *or*
www.gilliancross.co.uk

ROFL .... :-)) ... ROFL .. :-)) .. ROFL ..

Now read on for a taste of the fabulous new Demon Headmaster book:

Facing the Demon Headmaster

Chapter 1

Purple

'Ellie's completely changed since she started going to Purple!' Mandy said breathlessly. 'She says it's the most fantastic club there's ever been, and the DJ's brilliant! She wants to take us next time!'

All six members of SPLAT were sitting in Ian's lounge, drinking milk shakes. Mandy looked round at them, her face pink and eager.

'Well?' she said. 'Shall we go?'

How can a club be that great? thought Dinah. She didn't know Mandy's cousin Ellie, but she knew Mandy very well. And it took a lot to get her so excited. Was it really worth going to this Purple thing—whatever it was? Dinah glanced at the other four, to see what they were thinking.

Lloyd and Harvey—her two adopted brothers—had quite different expressions. Harvey was beaming, but Lloyd looked cautious. He wouldn't give a lead until he knew what everyone thought.

Ingrid was grinning and blowing bubbles down her straw. 'Let's make it a SPLAT outing! On Wednesday. That's the next Under Eighteens night, isn't it?'

Lloyd nodded, but he was still being cautious. He looked at Ian. 'What do you think?'

Ian leaned back in his chair, stretching out his long legs. 'I'm not *desperately* keen,' he drawled. 'But I'll go along with the rest of you, of course, if that's what we're doing.'

Lloyd was counting heads. 'We've got three in favour—Mandy and Harvey and Ingrid—and two of us who aren't sure. What about you, Di? Fancy a visit to Purple?'

Dinah frowned. 'I don't know anything about it. What's it like? Are all the walls purple, or something?'

'Of course not!' Ingrid said scornfully.

'So why is it called Purple?' said Dinah.

Shut up! Lloyd and Harvey both pulled faces at Dinah. *Don't be embarrassing!* But once Dinah started asking questions about something, she went on until she understood.

'Do you have to wear purple to get in?' she said.

Lloyd sighed and Harvey put his hands over his face.

'Where do you *live*? In a box?' Ingrid rolled her eyes up at the ceiling. 'Purple's been all over the television for weeks. In every magazine. Plastered across the newspapers. There are clubs opening up everywhere.'

Dinah shrugged. 'Well, I've been busy. There's lots of new research coming out about the socio-biology of feelings and facial expression—'

All the others groaned, and Lloyd threw a cushion at her to make her shut up.

'Who cares about science?' Ingrid growled.

Mandy reached over and patted her shoulder. 'Calm down, Ing. You can't expect a genius like Di to be interested in clubs.'

'Don't see why not,' Ingrid muttered. 'I thought science was about the real world. Purple's part of that. We've got to know about it!'

'She's right, Di.' Lloyd nodded, making up his mind. 'I vote for checking it out—and that makes four in favour. We'll have a SPLAT outing on Wednesday.'

'Fine,' said Dinah.

She wasn't going to argue any more now they'd voted. She might not care much about clubs, but SPLAT meant a lot to her. The Society for the Protection of our Lives Against Them. They were her best friends in the world and the six of them had been through a lot together. Battling against the sinister Headmaster and his plans to control the world had led them into all kinds of problems and dangers and they knew they could rely on each other. They were SPLAT and they stuck together.

*To find out more about SPLAT and about the strange new club Purple, read on in **Facing the Demon Headmaster**.*

DISCLAIMER

TABLE OF CONTENTS

SNACKS

Hummus & Veggie Dippers

Makes about 4 servings

Ingredients

1 can of garbanzo beans (chickpeas) rinsed and strained

¼ cup lemon juice (fresh squeezed, no pulp)

3 cloves of garlic, minced

¼ cup tahini

2 Tbs olive oil (organic)

1-2 tsp sea salt (to taste)

3 Tbs water

Veggie Sticks of choice (Celery, Peppers, Carrots, Zucchini, etc.)

Directions

In a magic bullet or food processor, mix the tahini and lemon juice for about a minute, then scrape the sides down and process another 45 seconds, you want a smooth, creamy texture. Add in the oil, garlic and salt. Mix for about 30-45 seconds and then scrape again. Mix another 30 seconds.

Add half of the beans to the mix and blend for about 1 minute, then scrape the sides. Add the other half and then mix for about 2 minutes until you have a thicker, creamier mixture. If you have the perfect texture now, voila! If not, add water a bit at a time and mix until you have the perfect dippable texture.

This is a great dip for veggies, but also works as a healthy spread for sandwiches.

Nutritional Fact

Packing this snack in your lunch will give you high amounts of protein and low fat. This means that you will have an energy boost without the crash. Mixed with the vegetable dippers, this is the PERFECT 3pm pick-me-up at the office, instead of hitting the vending machine.

Maple Banana Granola Bars

Makes about 8 granola bars

Ingredients

½ cup almonds (chopped)

1 cup oats (old fashioned rolled…not instant)

2 Tbs white sesame seeds

1 Tbs chia seeds

¼ cup chocolate shavings

2 bananas, mashed (yellow, some brown spots are ok)

1 Tbs raw, organic honey

1 Tbs molasses

2 Tbs coconut oil

½ tsp vanilla extract

¼ cup cranberries (or blueberries)

Directions

In a large bowl, combine oats, nuts, chocolate shavings, and seeds. Set off to the side for later.

Preheat oven to 325°F and line a loaf tin with wax paper or parchment paper

In a medium bowl, mix all wet ingredients together. Then add the wet mixture to the dry mixture. Add in the berries and fold them in as to not crush them.

Put the batter in the loaf tin and spread to an even layer. Bake in the oven for 30-40 minutes or until you see a golden brown crisp. Remove from the oven and cool completely. Cut into bars or squares and keep in the refrigerator until ready to serve.

Nutritional Fact

Making your own granola bars ensures that you will have yummy snacking without having any of the preservatives or extra sugars that cause health issues. This will allow you to have a healthy energy boost at work, without feeling guilty.

Cinnamon Applesauce

Makes 6-8 servings

Ingredients

2 Pink Lady apples

2 Granny Smith apples

2 Fuji apples

1 tsp lemon juice

2 Tbs cinnamon

½ cup water

Directions

Add all ingredients to a large saucepan and bring to a boil. Once boiling, reduce heat and lower to a simmer. Cover the pan, leaving a crack for air and cook for about 30 minutes. You want tender fruit…so adjust timing to accommodate.

Put the contents of the pot into a magic bullet, processor or blender. Puree until you have the consistency you desire (I like a few apple chunks, some like perfectly smooth.)

Nutritional Fact

For added nutrient value, leave the apple peels on as there are many vitamins, minerals, and fiber. Also, when shopping for apples, be sure to buy from the local farmers market—not only do you support local growers, but you also get the local nutrients that help with seasonal allergy immunity. If you need to sweeten, please use raw honey. It adds nutrients without preservatives.

Kale Chips

Makes approx. 4 servings

Ingredients

1 head of kale, ribs removed and cut into 1.5 inch strips

2-3 Tbs olive oil

Sea salt

Directions

In a medium bowl, place the kale pieces and pour in the olive oil. Sprinkle sea salt and then toss the kale to coat. Sprinkle more salt if necessary. Toss until each piece is coated and salted.

Spread out on a non-stick baking sheet and bake in a 275°F oven for approximately 20 minutes. You must turn halfway through to ensure crispy chips.

Nutritional Fact

Kale is loaded with so many vitamins it must taste gross, right? Wrong—baked and salted, this will curb your strongest craving for potato chips or pretzels.

Without the carbohydrate factor, you will not feel guilty when you eat more than one serving.

Popcorn Snack

Makes 5-6 servings

Ingredients

      1 cup white popcorn kernels
      2 Tbs coconut oil
      1 cup raisins or dried cranberries
      1 Tbs brown sugar
      2 tsp Sea Salt
      ½ cup milk chocolate chips

Directions

Pop in the coconut oil. In a small bowl, combine salt & sugar. Sprinkle mixture over corn as soon as it's done popping. Add in the fruit and chocolate and mix (toss) until well combined.

Nutritional Fact

Popcorn has less fat and calories than potato chips; therefore, it will satisfy the salty-snack desire without adding the grease and fat.

WRAPS

PB&J Banana Wraps

Makes 4 servings

Ingredients

Plantain Wraps

> 1 Large green plantain
> 2 Eggs
> 2 Tbs cold water
> 2 Tbs olive oil (extra virgin)
> 1/8 tsp sea salt
> Olive oil for frying

Filling

> 2 medium bananas (cut in half)
> 4 Tbs Organic Peanut Butter (tastes good with any nut butter)
> 4 Tbs of your favorite jam/jelly (organic, all natural, no sugar added)
> 1 tsp cinnamon

Directions

Peel plantain and place them in a blender or bullet with the remaining ingredients. You want to blend the mixture until it is smooth like pancake mix, maybe a little bit thicker.

In a medium skillet, preheat some olive oil and make your wraps just like you would a pancake- though you will notice it getting dry not bubbly. This is when you flip and finish the other side. Usually you cook for roughly 1-1 ½ minutes.

Pull off heat, and place on plate and set aside.

Take one wrap, and spread the PB&J all over. Sprinkle the cinnamon over top. Place a half banana in the middle. Roll up the wrap and enjoy!

Nutritional Fact

Plantains have loads of fiber, so using them to make your wraps will help cut out extra gluten and carbs that will only pack on pounds. This is a healthy, delicious wrap that will make you think differently about childhood favorites.

Avocado Chicken Wrap

Makes 4 servings

Use the <u>plantain wrap</u> recipe.

Ingredients

    1lb chicken breast, cut into strips
    1 avocado, chunks
    1 onion, thinly sliced
    1 tomato, sliced
    2 cup spinach leaves
    3 Tbs olive oil
    1 clove garlic, minced
    1 tsp fresh parsley, chopped
    Sea Salt & Pepper

Directions

In a large skillet, heat 2Tbs oil over medium heat. Add chicken, garlic and parsley and cook chicken thoroughly. Remove from heat, and set aside.

In a medium bowl, combine vegetables and salt & pepper. Toss with olive oil to coat.

On a wrap, place ¼ of the cooked chicken. Then add some of the salad mixture. Wrap up and enjoy!

For an added kick, spread a bit of the homemade hummus on the wrap before adding the chicken. Yum!

Nutritional Fact

Avocado is great for your skin and hair, so add it to your menu a few times a week.

Dijon Ham Wrap

Makes 1 serving, quick enough to make as you go.

Ingredients

> 1 Flour tortilla or a wrap of your choice
> 2 slices of ham (I prefer to make a ham and
> slice it, over buying deli meat, but it is your
> choice.)
> 1 slice of aged Swiss cheese
> 1 dollop of honey Dijon mustard
> 1 crisp lettuce leaf or a small handful of
> spinach

Directions

On the flat wrap, place the ham and then spread on
the mustard. This way it doesn't make the wrap soggy
in your lunch box. Add cheese and veggies of choice
(I like this wrap simple with a little lettuce.) and wrap it
up.

When you get to work, you can pop it in the
microwave for a few seconds to melt the cheese (I
remove the lettuce when I do this, but you don't have
to.) You can also grill these and serve them hot, but

this is difficult for a lunch box. They are delicious cold, served just as is.

Nutritional Fact

When choosing the correct wrap for your "wrap" you have plenty of options. Don't let this scare you. You want to add to the flavor of the filling, without diminishing by having a wrap made of ingredients you don't like. There are all kinds of wrap options: gluten free (plantain, for example) to whole wheat. There are ones made of spinach or tomatoes and then there is the ever popular, flour tortilla. Whichever you choose, be sure it's soft, flavorful and sticks to your diet of choice.

Crab and Cream Cheese Wrap

Makes 1 serving.

Ingredients

1 Flour tortilla or a wrap of your choice
¼ cup of flaked crab meat
2 Tbs cream cheese
1 Tbs mayonnaise
1 tsp of chopped onion
¼ tsp cayenne pepper
Pinch of garlic salt
1 crisp lettuce leaf or a small handful of spinach

Directions

Combine crab with cream cheese, mayonnaise.

Mix in chopped onion and salt and pepper.

On the flat wrap spread the crab mixture and place the salad mixture on top. Wrap up, cool in the refrigerator and enjoy!

Nutritional Fact

Crab is a natural source of omega 3 fatty acids which has been shown to have many health benefits. These include lowering inflammation in the body, lowering levels of depression and lowering blood fats that put you at risk for heart disease.

BLTA Wrap

This is a single serving recipe, but feel free to fry up a pound of bacon and make as many as you can. They freeze well for easy lunch options on busy mornings.

Ingredients

> 1 Wrap (I prefer the spinach/wheat one for this particular recipe)
> 2 -3 slices of crispy bacon
> Handful of sliced iceberg lettuce (feel free to substitute your favorite greens.)
> 2 tomato slices
> 3-4 avocado "strips" (peel, and slice in long thin strips)
> Optional: 1 dollop of mustard, ranch dressing, or sauce of your choice.

Directions

Compile ingredients on top of the spinach wrap. I like to squirt the mustard over the bacon, and then add the rest of the ingredients.

This wrap I enjoy cold, but I made one for my co-worker and she took half home. She decided to grill it and told me it was amazing. To each his own.

Nutritional Information

Bacon is good for you in moderation. Not only does it provide ample protein, but it also is a good source of B vitamins. This is why it makes such a great morning food, because it pumps you up for the day. Lunch as well, because everyone needs a lunch boost when you must work a full day.

SALADS

Avocado Steak Salad

Makes 3-4 servings

Ingredients

> 1 sirloin steak (approx. 1lb and 1 inch thick)
> 1/3 cup low sodium soy sauce
> 4 Tbs olive oil
> 1 head romaine lettuce (small, chopped)
> ½ cup cilantro (fresh, chopped)
> Crumbles of Feta cheese (small handful)
> 1 red onion (finely sliced)
> 1 avocado (peeled and sliced)
> 3 Tbs lime juice
> Sea Salt & Pepper to taste

Directions

Set aside the steak in a medium bowl with the soy sauce for roughly 30-40 minutes to marinade.

In a large frying pan, heat 2 Tsp of oil and cook the steak until done (rare, medium rare, medium, well, etc.)

When the steak has finished cooking, set it aside to cool for 5 minutes. Slice in thin strips across.

In a medium bowl, add the remaining ingredients (except the salt & pepper) and toss together. Add the steak on top and salt to taste.

For lunches—you can make the steak ahead and then compile the salad one serving at a time if you prefer so that it is fresh every day.

Nutritional Fact

Cilantro has many health benefits, and it isn't used nearly enough. High in vitamins A, C, and K, and rich in iron, this is an easy addition to your diet that will make a huge difference in how you look and feel.

Mandarin Chicken Salad

Makes 4 servings

Ingredients

> 1 head of romaine lettuce, chopped (approx. 10oz)
> 1 lb. cooked chicken, shredded
> 3-4 mandarin oranges, peeled and segmented
> ¼ cup dried cranberries, no sugar added
> ¼ cup orange juice
> 1 tsp Dijon mustard
> 1 Tbs avocado oil
> 1 tsp garlic powder
> 2 tsp raw organic honey
> Sea salt

Directions

In a large mixing bowl, mix together lettuce, chicken, oranges, and cranberries. Set aside.

In a small mixing bowl, add the rest of the ingredients together and whisk until you have a well-mixed dressing. Keep in a separate container when packing lunch and add right before eating. Toss and enjoy!

Nutritional Fact

This is a delicious lunch salad, great for a mood lifter as Vitamin C and oranges in general help to promote happiness. Load up on the oranges, and snack often!

Strawberry Chicken Salad

Makes 4 servings

Ingredients

> ½ quart of strawberries, halved and cored
> 1 lb. cooked chicken, shredded
> 2 cups baby spinach
> 2 cups romaine lettuce, chopped
> 1 red onion, sliced
> ½ avocado, chunks
> 1/3 cup chopped walnuts
> ¼ cup feta cheese
> 3 Tbs avocado oil
> 1 tsp lemon juice
> 1 tsp lime juice
> Sea Salt

Directions

In a medium mixing bowl, combine the first eight ingredients and set aside.

In a small mixing bowl, whisk together the oil, juice and salt. Store in a separate container for lunches, and add right before eating. Toss together and enjoy!

Nutritional Fact

Eating strawberries three times a week can have great anti-inflammatory benefits on your body. If you find yourself in serious pain often, add a dose of strawberry goodness, and see what happens!

Tuna Salad

Makes 5 servings

Ingredients

   1 ½ lb tuna steaks, 1 inch thick
   2Tbs Olive Oil
   1Tbs lemon juice
   1Tbs garlic, minced
   6 cups chopped romaine lettuce/mixed salad greens
   1 yellow onion, sliced
   1 handful cherry tomatoes
   1 green bell pepper, sliced
   2 Tbs parmesan cheese

Directions

In a bowl, add steaks, oil, ½ Tbs lemon juice and garlic—marinate in refrigerator for 20 minutes.

On an outdoor grill, grill plate, or other similar option, set heat to medium-high and oil the surface.

Grill the tuna steaks for about 5 minutes each side, sprinkling the remaining lemon juice over top. Cook until its light in color and pink in center.

Set aside for about 5 minutes while you prepare the salad.

In a large mixing bowl, add lettuce and other veggies and toss together.

Slice the tuna steaks into strips, and place on top of the salad. Sprinkle with parmesan cheese and serve.

For lunches, you can cook steaks ahead of time and prepare the salad day of.

I prefer no dressing on this salad, but if you would like a dressing—it's great with a light oil and vinegar or even an Italian dressing.

Nutritional Fact

Anti-inflammatory and antioxidant benefits of eating tuna weekly will be highly appreciated. You need the omega-3 fatty acids, to help support brain and muscle function and cell regeneration. Eat up!

SANDWICHES

Caesar Salad Sandwich

Makes 2 servings

Ingredients

> 1 cup romaine lettuce chopped
> 6 oz. grilled chicken strips
> ½ cup Caesar dressing
> ¼ cup Asiago parmesan cheese
> ½ small purple onion, diced
> 4 cherry tomatoes, halved
> 4 slices of pumpernickel bread

Directions

In a medium mixing bowl, toss lettuce, ¼ cup dressing, and veggies together. Set aside.

Spread some dressing on 2 slices of bread. Add a scoop of the salad mixture, place 3oz of chicken strips over each slice and sprinkle with ½ of the cheese. Cover with the dry slice of bread, and enjoy!

Nutritional Fact

Did you know that Caesar dressing is made with anchovies? This may turn some people off, but don't let it… the dressing tastes great no matter what. With this addition to the mix, it also adds protein, essential fatty acids and other vitamins. Be sure to get a low-fat version of the dressing.

Avocado Chicken Salad Sandwich

Makes 4-6 servings

Ingredients

>3 Avocado
>1 Tbs lemon juice
>1 lb. cooked, shredded chicken
>2 Tbs dill spice
>2 Stalk of celery, diced
>1 purple onion, diced
>Sea Salt
>Black Pepper
>6 Slices of your favorite bread (for this sandwich, I enjoy Rye)

Directions

You will make this just like you would make a "chicken salad" out of mayonnaise. Instead of slathering on mayo, you will mash the ingredients together with avocado.

In a medium bowl, mash the peeled avocados until moderately smooth. Add the lemon juice and continue to mash. Salt and Pepper to taste. Add your shredded chicken, and vegetables. Finally, add the spices and mix all together.

On a piece of bread, add any lettuce or tomato if desired, and a scoop of the prepared chicken salad. Cover with the other slice of bread, and enjoy!

Nutritional Fact

Mayonnaise is loaded with fat and excess calories, but until now, it has been difficult to make any of the popular salads without it. Now, you can involve avocado and all of its nutrients to make your favorite salads and enjoy them without guilt. Try a tuna salad, potato salad, and more. Get creative!

Gourmet PB&J

Makes 1 serving

Ingredients

>   2 slices of pumpernickel bread
>   1 Tbs peanut butter, creamy
>   1 Tbs raspberry jam (or your favorite)
>   1 sprinkle pumpkin pie spice
>   ½ banana, thinly sliced

Directions

On one slice of bread, spread the peanut butter and sprinkle the pumpkin spice over top.

On the other side, spread the jelly, and lay out the banana slices.

Combine both sides, and prepare for an "Aha" moment. Childhood favorite hacked into an amazingly delicious and healthy grown-up sandwich!

Nutritional Fact

Bananas are health food GOLD, boosting your mood, energy, and helping to ward off muscle cramps and spasms.

Pizza Croissant Roll Ups

Makes 8 roll ups

Ingredients

> 1 package croissant dough (I use Pillsbury in the recipe, you can use store brand or make your own dough for a gluten free variation)
> 3 Tbs pizza sauce
> 1 tsp garlic powder
> 4 mozzarella string cheese sticks (cut in half)
> 2 Tbs butter, melted

Directions

Lay out the croissants on a non-stick (or sprayed) cookie sheet. Mix the garlic powder into the melted butter and brush over each croissant.

Spoon pizza sauce onto each croissant and spread about halfway down.

Lay ½ of a cheese stick at the top (large) end of the croissant dough. Roll up from there.

Brush each with the garlic butter.

Bake according to package directions. (or 375°F for about 8-10 minutes) until golden brown and cheese is melted.

Refrigerate in separate packages for easy lunch packing. When ready to eat, pop in microwave for about 20 seconds or so.

Nutritional Fact

Garlic is a natural antibiotic, if you can use it somewhere, DO. Be liberal with it, and use it often-especially during cold and flu season.

SOUPS

Loaded Baked Potato Soup

Makes 4-6 servings

Ingredients

> 2 Idaho potatoes, peeled & cubed
> 4 red potatoes, peeled & halved
> 6 Slices cooked bacon, crumbled
> ½ cup beef broth
> 2 cups water
> 1 cup sharp cheddar cheese, shredded
> ½ cup Asiago cheese, shredded
> 1 head cauliflower, center stalk removed
> 2 cloves garlic, peeled
> ½ cup coconut milk (heavy cream if you don't mind the calories)
> ½ cup cream cheese, softened
> Sea Salt and Black Pepper to taste

Directions

In a large sauce pan, boil/steam the cauliflower until soft (about 15-20 minutes) strain and add to food processor. Also add in garlic, milk, cream cheese and ¼ cup beef broth. Puree until smooth. Set aside.

In a large pot, add potatoes, remaining broth and water. Cook until the potatoes are 50 % cooked. Add in the cream soup base and continue cooking over medium heat until potatoes are tender. Add in the shredded cheeses a little at a time, and let it melt as you stir it in. Finally mix in the bacon and continue to cook on med-low for another 30 minutes. Salt and Pepper to taste if needed.

Nutritional Fact

Cream soups can be loaded with excess fats and calories. Using a cream cauliflower base adds in vitamins and minerals while cutting out the fat. This soup   will   be   healthy   and   taste   decadent.

French Onion

Makes 4-6 servings

Ingredients

> 6-7 yellow onions, peeled and sliced
> 2 cloves of garlic, minced
> ½ stick salted butter
> 12 oz. beef stock
> 8 cups of water
> 1 Tbs Worcestershire sauce
> 1 tsp ketchup
> 2 tsp Sea Salt
> 1 tsp black pepper
> 1 tsp dried thyme
> Baguette (1-2 depending on size)
> 6 Slices Asiago (or Swiss, or parmesan) cheese
> 1 cup croutons (you can make your own by baking some chopped bread brushed with garlic butter)

Directions

In a large pot, place butter on medium-high heat to melt. Add garlic and onions once butter is melted. Cook for 7-10 minutes on med-high heat, mixing enough not to burn the onions. Then reduce to medium and continue cooking until onions cook down and are tender. Add the Worcestershire sauce and ketchup and thyme, and mix in while cooking onions. Simmer on medium for another 10-15 minutes.

Add beef stock and simmer on med-low for 35 minutes. Add in water, salt & pepper and cook for at least another hour.

For lunches, cut 1 inch slices of baguette. In a zip loc bag, add a handful of croutons, 1 slice of cheese and a slice baguette. When ready to prepare, in a soup bowl, drop in the croutons, add soup, place cheese over top, melt in microwave for about 1 minute. Then use the baguette to dip. (This is an optional step as some prefer baguette OR croutons. I like both.)

Nutritional Fact

Onions and garlic both are great for the heart. They allow for better circulation and healthier levels of cholesterol.

Creamy Chicken Soup

Makes 4-6 servings

Ingredients

    1 head cauliflower, center stalk removed
    1 lb. cooked chicken, cut into chunks
    1 carrot sliced
    1 stalk celery
    1 yellow onion, chopped
    1 cup chicken stock
    1 cup vegetable stock
    2 cloves garlic, peeled
    1 cup uncooked rice
    2 cups original coconut milk
    Sea Salt & Pepper

Directions

In a large pot, combine the stock and vegetables and begin to cook on medium heat for about 30 minutes.

In a large saucepan, boil/steam the cauliflower until soft (about 15-20 minutes) strain.

In a food processor, add the cauliflower, 1 cup milk, and garlic. Puree until smooth. Add this mixture to the large pot with vegetables and the other cup of milk. Continue to cook on medium for 25 minutes.

Add in rice and chicken, and cook another 25-30 minutes. Salt and pepper to taste. Remove from heat and store in separate containers for easy lunch packing.

Nutritional Fact

Chicken soup really is good for the soul! A combination of vegetables, broth and protein helps to boost the immune system and mood when you are cold or feeling under the weather.

Black Bean Chili

Makes 4 servings

Ingredients

> 1 yellow onion, chopped
> 1 green bell pepper, diced
> 1 red bell pepper, diced
> 2 cups vegetable broth
> 5 cloves garlic, chopped
> 1 cup fresh corn
> 4 cups of black beans (drained if using canned)
> 1 cup tomato sauce
> 1 lb. diced tomatoes
> 2 Tbs ground cumin
> 2 Tbs paprika
> ¼ cup fresh oregano, finely chopped
> ¼ cup fresh cilantro, chopped
> Sea Salt
> Black Pepper

Directions

Warm on medium heat, 1 Tbs of vegetable broth in a large soup pan. Sauté the onion and peppers for about 5 minutes. You want them to be tender, so stir often and check texture. Once tender, add spices, and continue to sauté for about 2 minutes.

Add remaining broth and the remaining ingredients, except corn. Simmer for about 20 more minutes. Add corn, salt and pepper to taste, and continue to cook for 2 minutes, stirring often.

Remove from heat and serve, or dish into separate containers for easy packing.

Nutritional Fact

Beans offer an amazing amount of fiber and minerals. This soup is loaded with nutrients, and it tastes delicious. You can adjust the spices to suit your level of temperature desired, but feel free to add in jalapeños or other vegetables as well.

CONCLUSION

You have just received the gift of knowledge. Knowing that you can make delicious, nutritious, and quick meals for your lunch box gives you a one up on the competition. While your co-workers are spending extra dollars eating out, or scrambling in the early mornings to pack their lunch, you are sitting pretty knowing that your box is filled with health.

Whether you are a soup and sandwich person, or a salad fiend, you have seen many recipes in this book that should grab your interest. As I said before, be sure to mark your favorites for quick use, but also give everything a shot—there are great salad options that you maybe never would have thought about. Our taste buds change so often that we can try new foods regularly and finds new favorites. However, our mental tastes don't often forget, so if there is a recipe that uses something you may not have enjoyed in the past—forget about it. Try the recipe with a new excitement and open mind. You may be surprised at what you will like when you give is a positive chance.

13859598R00028

Printed in Great Britain
by Amazon